For Michael Philip
J. C.

For Amelia
S. L.

First published by Candlewick Press.

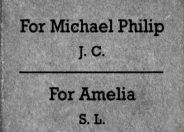

CANDLEWICK PRESS
2067 MASSACHUSETTS AVENUE
CAMBRIDGE MA 02140

ISBN 0-590-99641-X

Text copyright © 1995 by June Crebbin. Illustrations copyright
© 1995 by Stephen Lambert. All rights reserved. Published by Scholastic
Inc., 555 Broadway, New York, NY 10012, by arrangement with
Candlewick Press.

12 11 10 9 8 7 6   9/9 0 1 2/0

Printed in the U.S.A.   08

First Scholastic printing, March 1997

The pictures in this book were done in chalk pastel.

The Train Ride

illustrated by

June Crebbin   CANDLEWICK PRESS
CAMBRIDGE, MASSACHUSETTS   **Stephen Lambert**

We're off on a journey   Out of the town –

What shall I see?   What shall I see?

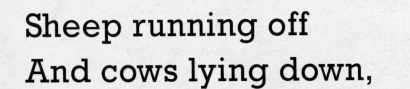

Sheep running off
And cows lying down,

That's what I see,
That's what I see.

Over the meadow,
Up on the hill,

What shall I see?
What shall I see?

A mare and her foal
Standing perfectly still,

That's what I see,
That's what I see.

There is a farm
Down a bumpety road —

What shall I see?
What shall I see?

A shiny red tractor
Pulling its load,

That's what I see,
That's what I see.

Here in my seat,
My lunch on my knee,

What shall I see?
What shall I see?

A ticket collector
Smiling at me,

That's what I see,
That's what I see.

Into the tunnel,
Scary and black,

What shall I see?
What shall I see?

My face in a mirror,
Staring back,

That's what I see,
That's what I see.

After the tunnel,
When we come out,

What shall I see?
What shall I see?

A gaggle of geese
Strutting about,

That's what I see,
That's what I see.

Over the treetops,   What shall I see?
High in the sky,   What shall I see?

A giant balloon
Sailing by,

That's what I see,
That's what I see.

Listen! The engine
Is slowing down —

What shall I see?
What shall I see?

A market square,
A seaside town,

That's what I see,
That's what I see.

There is the lighthouse,   The sand, and the sea . .

Here is the station —

Whom shall I see?

There is my grandma

Welcoming me . . .

Welcoming

me.